Shivers™

A WAKING NIGHTMARE

M. D. Spenser

Plantation, Florida

To my sister Sue,
and
John, Jessie, Erin and Seth

This book may not be reproduced in whole or in part, or stored in any type of retrieval system, or transmitted in any way or via any means: electronic, mechanical, photocopying, or recording without permission of the publisher.

Copyright © 1996 by M.D. Spenser. All rights reserved.

Published by Paradise Press, Inc. by arrangement with River Publishing, Inc. All right, title and interest to the "SHIVERS" logo and design are owned by River Publishing, Inc. No portion of the "SHIVERS" logo and design may be reproduced in part or whole without prior written permission from River Publishing, Inc. An application for a registered trademark of the "SHIVERS" logo and design is pending with the Federal Patent and Trademark office.

ISBN 1-57657-100-9
30621

EXCLUSIVE DISTRIBUTION BY PARADISE PRESS, INC.

Cover Design by George Paturzo

Cover Illustration by Eddie Roseboom

Printed in the U.S.A.

Chapter One

I hate getting blamed for things I didn't do. It makes me mad.

So I was none too happy that morning when I woke up to hear my mother yelling my name.

"Mar-*tin!*" she yelled. I could tell by her voice that she was angry at me about something.

The thing was that I couldn't have done anything. I hadn't even gotten out of bed yet, for Pete's sake. My feet hadn't even touched the floor. How could I have messed up already?

"What?" I yelled.

Mom's voice bounded up the stairway, around the hallway and into my room, angrier than ever.

"Mar-*tin!*" she yelled. "You get down here this

minute!"

Reluctantly, I peeled off my covers, sat up, and rubbed my hands through my hair. I knew it was sticking up. It always does in the morning.

I planted my feet on the cold wooden floor and stood up. I wondered what the heck was I going to be accused of now.

I felt really sleepy, more tired than I should have. I had gone to bed at a reasonable enough hour — and slept like a log, too. I hadn't woken up once.

I looked at my clock. It said 9:30. Mom had let me sleep late, since it was summer. Or, more likely, she had slept late herself.

Still, I felt awfully tired. I yawned and fell back into the bed to catch one more little doze.

"Mar-*tin!*"

I jumped out of bed, then stood stock still in the middle of the floor while I tried to figure out where the heck I was. I had stood up too fast and nearly blacked out. I mean, I knew I was standing, and I knew who I was and where I was. I just couldn't *see* anything. For about ten seconds I was afraid that, if I took a step, I'd fall down or bump into something.

"*Mar*-tin!"

Uh-oh. My mom is nice and patient most of the time. But when she starts putting the accent on the first syllable of my name, that means she's really angry.

I padded down the stairs in my bare feet and wrinkled pajamas.

Mom was standing in the middle of the kitchen in her bathrobe, with her hands on her hips. Her lips were pursed into a straight line. Her eyes were puffy — obviously, she had just woken up herself — and her hair stood up on end.

We probably looked ridiculous, I thought, each of us standing there with our hair on end. But Mom did not look as if she saw the humor in much of anything just then.

"Martin," she said, and glared at me. "Number one . . . "

Oh, no, I thought. We've got a list. How could

I possibly have committed a whole list of crimes this early in the morning?

"When dinner is over, we do not eat any more for the rest of the day," Mom said. "That's the rule, and you know it."

I squinted at her, perplexed.

"But, Mom . . . "

"Number two," she continued. "*If* you have to eat something, then ask me. I will tell you what you can have."

"But, Mom . . ."

"Number three," she said. "*If* you feel an irresistible urge to violate the rules and eat something, the very *least* you could do is clean up after yourself."

"But, Mom," I said. "I didn't eat anything."

"Don't even start, Martin," she said. "Give me a little more credit than that. When there's peanut butter involved, I know it's you. Look at this mess! It looks as if you deliberately spread peanut butter all over the sink."

She took one hand off her hip and pointed. I

looked. There certainly was peanut butter spread all over the sink, thick globs of it smeared everywhere.

Without a word, Mom pointed at the floor.

A spoon, goopy with peanut butter, was stuck to the linoleum.

She pointed at the counter. An empty peanut butter jar lay on its side.

I could not figure this out. My face felt like it was hanging out in front of me, looking stupid.

"Don't try to put on that bewildered expression," Mom said. "That was a new jar last Tuesday. How much did you eat? What did you do — just ladle the stuff straight out of the jar and into your mouth?"

My face hung out even further in front of me, and looked even dumber. I could feel it.

I heard a shuffling noise. I turned and saw my little brother, Farley, standing at the foot of the stairs. That embarrassed me. I didn't want him to think things were always like this around here, with me in trouble and getting yelled at.

I was starting to get mad.

"Mom, I did not do this," I snapped.

"And what about this?" she asked, pulling a broken plate from the bottom of the sink. It was a nice pottery plate, from a set I think Mom and Dad had been given when they got married. "What did you do, toss it from across the room like it was a Frisbee?"

"MOM!" I shouted. "Listen to me! I did not do this!"

"Martin," Mom said quietly. "You are making me very angry. Very, *very* angry. Don't say another word. Do not eat anything more after dinner. Ever. Just clean this up right now so we can go to the ocean, as we planned."

"I will not clean it up!" I shouted. "I did not make this mess! I will *not* clean it up! It's *not* my fault!"

"*Then . . . go . . . to . . . your . . . room . . . this . . . minute,*" Mom said, biting off each word like a piece off a carrot. "This mess is staying just as it is, and no one is going anywhere until *you* decide to come down clean it up."

Chapter Two

I stormed up the stairs to my room and slammed the door. As I said, I hate getting blamed for things I haven't done.

At first I just sat on my bed and steamed and stewed about the injustice of it all. It was so unfair. Mom had not even listened to me.

And I was definitely not going to clean up a mess I had not made.

But after a while, I started to puzzle over the whole thing. It was peculiar. I would have been happy to blame someone else for the mess, but I couldn't figure out who else could have made it.

It certainly wasn't Mom. She was very neat — plus she hated peanut butter.

It couldn't have been Farley. He can be pretty messy, when he puts his mind to it, but he always admits it whenever he does something wrong. Once I even got him to confess to something *I* had done.

That was a year ago, when he was seven and I was eleven.

I can't remember what I'd done wrong that time, but it was something bad. Dad was conducting a huge investigation.

Farley and I were both denying whatever it was. The main difference was that Farley was denying it because he hadn't done it, and I was denying it because I didn't feel like admitting it and getting punished.

So we were both getting sent to our rooms. On the way up the stairs, I whispered to Farley out of the side of my mouth. I think I promised him I'd be nice to him the whole rest of the day if he would own up to what I'd done, and he did.

I stood on the stairs and watched Dad ream him out.

“So you were willing to see your brother get punished for something you had really done,” Dad said to Farley.

The little guy just hung his head and mumbled. Then he got sent to his room by himself.

I still felt bad about having persuaded him to do that. He’s a nice kid. I miss him during the winter-time, when he’s not around.

I never really got the chance to apologize to him. I don’t think it was very long afterwards that Mom and Dad got divorced, and Dad moved out of here and got a house in Phoenix, Arizona. Arizona is a long way away from Maine, which is where Mom and I live.

I stayed with Mom. Farley went to live with Dad.

We didn’t choose to have it that way, but it didn’t really cause a problem. Farley and I spend all our vacation time together — Christmas, spring break, and summer vacation. We spend half the time at Mom’s house, and half the time at Dad’s.

I figured we got along better than if we lived together all the time. We didn't have so much time to get on each other's nerves.

Everybody at school kept asking me if I was upset or mad about Mom and Dad getting divorced. I wasn't.

Actually, it was kind of cool. It made me different from the other kids. It gave me something to talk about where the other kids would all listen with their mouths open.

The way I saw it, having my parents divorced made me a smarter person, more mature, you might say. Other kids just heard what their parents told them and automatically believed it. The children of Baptists were always Baptists. The kids with conservative parents were conservative. The kids with liberal parents were liberal.

My parents told me different things — *way* different things — so I had to pick and choose and decide for myself what I wanted to believe.

It gave me more judgment. It made me a little

more independent in my thinking. That was good, not something to be mad or upset about.

As I sat there in my room, I decided to use that judgment and maturity just a little bit.

Next chance I got, I would remember to tell Farley I was sorry that I convinced him to get punished for something I'd done. I really did feel bad about that.

Chapter Three

After a while, I started reading a book.

I wasn't mad any more, but I certainly wasn't going to go downstairs and clean up a mess I hadn't made. I figured I did enough bad stuff on my own. I didn't have to take responsibility for bad stuff I didn't do.

Besides, sitting in my room was boring.

And I read a lot, anyway.

I read when I'm mad, to calm myself down. I read when I'm happy, because I enjoy it. I read when I'm sad, to take my mind off my troubles. I read when I can't fall asleep. I read when I'm bored.

In fact, I try to be careful not to go anywhere without a book, in case one of those things happens to me. One of them usually does.

This time, I was reading a book about the history of Australia. Other kids think I'm crazy to actually enjoy reading history, but I do. Did you know that the continent was colonized by criminals? It's true. Two hundred years ago, England decided it had too many criminals, and started shipping them off to Australia, which was the other end of the world in those days.

Come to think of it, it still *is* the other end of the world, if you live in Maine, likc I do.

Anyway, I was just getting to a good part, about a convicted criminal in Australia who was flogged so many times his collar bones stuck out of his skin permanently, when Farley snuck into my room.

He had brought some lunch — a sandwich for me, and a sandwich for him. That was nice of him, because I wasn't allowed to go out of my room, even to eat. He really is a good kid.

I remembered that I'd promised myself that I'd use some of that good judgment I'd gained recently.

"Farley," I said. "Remember that time I got you to tell Dad you'd done something, and really I had done it?"

"Yeah," he said matter-of-factly, and took a bite of his sandwich. "When you tried to drive Dad's car and backed it over Mom's bicycle. Boy, was Dad mad that time."

"Uh, maybe that was it," I said. "I've kind of forgotten what it was about."

Actually, I *had* kind of forgotten, but what Farley said brought it all back to me. I just didn't want to admit it.

I had backed the car over Mom's brand new shiny twelve-speed mountain bike, turning it into more of a shiny new metal pretzel than a bicycle. She had barged into the house, asking Dad why the heck didn't he look before he backed the car up. Dad had asked her why the heck she didn't ask what the situation was before she started yelling at him. They had yelled at each other a while. Then Dad had gotten mad at us.

"I just wanted to say," I told Farley, "that I'm

sorry I convinced you to say that you did it. That wasn't very nice of me, and I'm sorry." Farley seemed unconcerned.

"That's OK," he said, munching on his sandwich some more. "That must have been a year ago. No problem. I know you'd do the same for me sometime."

"Yeah," I said. "I would." But I wasn't so sure.

"By the way," Farley said, "Mom's out in the garden. I cleaned up the kitchen for you. All you have to do is say it was you, and you're free. Or at least don't deny that you cleaned up when Mom praises you for it."

"Aw, thank you, Bruddy," I said.

That was my nickname for him, because the name Farley struck me as stupid — and Farley was anything but stupid. Bruddy was my word for brother, and I loved having Farley for my brother.

I was really moved by what he'd done. It was nice that he cared that much about me, even after the family had been split up.

“Thanks,” I said again. “I really mean it.”

“That’s OK,” he said. “That way, you and me and Mom can all go to the ocean together tomorrow. I didn’t want our family trip to get wrecked.”

Chapter Four

I had a hard time going to sleep that night.

Maybe it was because I was excited about going to the ocean the next day. I love going to the ocean.

In Maine, at least in the part of Maine I live in, you can't really call it the beach. There's almost no sand. Big boulders jut grandly out into the blue of the ocean, and it's so beautiful it takes my breath away.

People say you tend to take the place where you grew up for granted, and you never really appreciate how beautiful it is because you're so used to it. That's not true for me.

Just the opposite, in fact. When I visit Arizona, which a lot of people say is great, it does nothing for me. It's just hot and dry — and not that pretty, if you ask me.

Everybody there says the heat doesn't bother them because there's no humidity, and the air's so dry, but I never heard anything so stupid in my life. The air in a blast furnace is dry, too, but I don't want to live in one.

Then when I get back to Maine, it takes my breath away all over again. I think the places where each of us grew up mean *more* to us than other places, not less. I think they remind us of when we were little and everything was great, and that's why we think they're even more beautiful than other people think they are.

Going to the ocean was always one of my favorite things. My dad used to take me and Farley swimming. He taught us how to get out past the place where the waves are breaking. That's where they're really scary — sheer, powerful walls of water with white foam curling over the top ready to dash you against the same rocks that remind you of your wonderful childhood.

You get past that point by diving right through the middle of the wall of water and coming out on the other side. Then you swim as fast as you can — and you might have to dive through the middle of another wave — until you're out beyond where the waves are breaking.

Out there, my dad showed me, the waves just roll on by. You bob up and down like a cork, floating up one side of an enormous mountain of water and sliding down the other side.

Dad always shouted, "Whoooooo," like he was on a roller coaster, just to teach us how to have fun.

I tossed and turned under the covers. I thought of pleasant things, like lying on a rock after a swim and dozing in the warm afternoon sun. But I still couldn't get to sleep.

Something besides excitement over going to the ocean with Mom and Farley was keeping me awake. And it was puzzlement.

I absolutely could not figure out who had made that horrible mess in the kitchen.

The more I thought about it, the more nervous I became.

There were only three of us in the house: Mom, Farley, and me.

Mom hadn't done it. That was obvious. She didn't spoon peanut butter into her mouth, break a dish in the sink, then walk off and leave everything that way.

And Farley hadn't done it. He confessed to everything he did, and some things he didn't do. Besides, Farley didn't even like peanut butter. He said it glued his tongue to the roof of his mouth and made it hard for him to breathe. He never ate peanut butter sandwiches. He was afraid that one day he'd get stuck with his tongue glued to his mouth, and then he'd die.

Murdered by a peanut butter sandwich.

And I knew darn well that I hadn't left that mess.

The way I figured it, that left only one conclusion. It was a conclusion I didn't like very much. It made me nervous. Even scared.

If none of *us* had made that mess, then someone *else* — an intruder — had snuck into our house while we were asleep.

Even if the intruder hadn't taken anything or hurt any of us, the idea frightened me. I like to feel safe in my own home. I like to think I'll wake up in the morning and everything will be just the same as it was the night before. I don't like to think that unknown people are tromping around wrecking things in my house while I'm asleep.

How could I ever convince Mom that an intruder had entered our house? It was important for her to know, because maybe we were in danger. But if I tried to tell her anything, she'd just get mad and say I was denying everything again, when I just really ought to say I'm sorry.

Worrying about all of that was keeping me awake. It gave me a nervous feeling in the pit of my stomach.

I sighed, pulled the covers off, got up and turned on the light. Clearly, I was not falling asleep right away tonight.

I walked around my room adjusting everything. Sometimes knowing that everything is exactly in its place helps me to feel more comfortable, and then I start nodding off. I don't know why.

I lined my CDs up on their shelf so they were exactly even with each other, and checked to make sure they were still alphabetized by artist. I lined my pencils up next to each other beside the blotter on my desk. I adjusted my diary, though I hadn't written anything in it in more than a year, so that its corner matched the corner of the desk.

I moved around the room, fixing this, adjusting that.

On the left side of my dresser, I slid the mug in which I keep my pocket stuff — my lucky penny, squashed flat by a train; whatever dollars I have; and my Swiss Army knife — into its proper position.

On the right side, I moved my house key into

its place. Mom had given me the key, just in case I ever had to let myself into the house.

"You're the man of the house now," she had said.

The framed picture of my family looked out of place. I like it in the exact center of the dresser top.

I picked it up to look at it. It was my favorite photograph. It showed the four of us on a summer vacation to Montana, at a place where we rode horses for a week. Snowcapped mountains loomed in the background. Farley and I stood in the foreground, wearing jeans and cowboy boots.

Mom and Dad stood right behind us. We were all smiling. Dad had his arm around Mom's shoulder.

I put the picture down carefully, so that it was precisely halfway between the wall and the front of the dresser, and halfway between the Swiss Army knife and my house key.

Then I picked up my book, turned on my reading lamp, turned off my ceiling light, and hopped back into bed.

Nothing like a little light reading, I thought, to take my mind off of scary things like peanut butter-eating intruders tromping around my house at night breaking plates.

That night I read about the voyages of death in the late 1700s, when they loaded creaky old ships with criminals and shipped them on the three-month journey from England to Australia. They kept the criminals locked below deck most of the time, where it was dark and smelly, and they fed the prisoners hardly anything at all.

The men fell sick and began to starve. Many of them died.

I fell asleep dreaming sweet dreams of criminals who wouldn't tell anyone when the man chained next to them died, so they could eat his food as well as their own.

Chapter Five

I woke up early the next morning. I felt sleepy again, though I had slept like a baby, without waking up once.

I guess dreaming about criminals starving on stinking ships hadn't been quite as restful as I'd hoped.

But I was excited about going to the ocean. I assume that's why I woke up so early.

I lay in bed a few minutes. I heard Mom walking around downstairs. I listened nervously.

Fortunately, I did *not* hear her yell "Mar-*tin!*"

I breathed a sigh of relief. Nothing was amiss. No peanut butter had been spread all over the place. No plates had been broken. The intruder had not returned. Everything was OK.

Happy, I scrambled out of bed and thundered down the stairs. Mom was standing at the counter cooking waffles. Syrup was warming on the stove. It smelled so sweet it made me twice as hungry as I already was.

Sunlight streamed in through the window. Mom looked up at me and smiled.

My mom is really beautiful, I thought to myself. I'm lucky to have her.

"Hungry?" she asked.

Was I ever!

Farley came down to the kitchen, and the two of us bolted down enough waffles to feed about fourteen people. Then we cleaned up, ran upstairs to pack our bathing suits, towels and flip flops, and barreled back downstairs.

Mom was still cleaning the kitchen, wiping the counters until they sparkled. She looked up and saw us panting, each holding our beach bags, and laughed.

"You boys aren't eager or anything, are you?" she asked. "Just give me a minute, and we'll be on our way."

She disappeared into her bedroom. Farley and I tapped our feet impatiently. She was probably in her room about three minutes, but to us it felt like half an hour.

Finally she emerged, wearing her bathing suit, dark glasses, and a straw hat with a big floppy brim. She had a book tucked under one arm. In her other hand, she carried her own beach bag.

She smiled and tousled my hair. I squirmed away from her. I like it when she does that, but I pretend not to. I am twelve years old, after all.

"Come on, boys," Mom said. "This will be a fun day."

She scooped up Skunk, our cat — we always leave her outside when we're going to be away for the day and we trooped outdoors into the sunny summer day.

A breeze stirred the leaves. Sunlight filtered through the woods and made little pools of light that danced across our driveway. It was a perfect day —

warm enough for us to swim, but not so hot we'd fry.

Then Mom gasped.

"Oh, no!" she cried.

She dropped her bag and circled the car, stooping down to look as she went.

When she stood up again, her face was white. She looked scared. I thought maybe she was going to cry.

But she didn't.

Instead she said, sharply, "Children, get inside."

I dropped my gaze to the bottom of the car, where she had been looking. Then I saw it, too.

The front left tire was flat. Mom stood there, frozen. I walked around the car, as she had done. My jaw dropped.

The car didn't have just one flat tire. All four tires were flat.

I bent down to take a look.

They were slashed. Someone flattened our tires on purpose, with a razor, perhaps, or a knife.

Chapter Six

"Children, get back inside," Mom said, and there was urgency in her voice.

We didn't have to be told twice. All right, we *did* have to be told twice, but we didn't have to be told three times, at any rate.

We realized this was serious. Someone had slashed our tires. Someone was after us.

There was no telling who had done it, or why, or when. Mom had used the car the evening before, to make a grocery run — buying more peanut butter, probably — and the tires had been fine then.

Had the attack come overnight? Could someone possibly have found his way up to our house in the woods in the dark of night?

Or had the tires been slashed this morning, while we had been savoring our waffles and syrup? Could the slasher be lurking in the woods right this minute, ready to jump out and attack us?

We were at his mercy. With the tires flat, we had no way to escape, no way to reach civilization. We were trapped in our house in the woods.

I cast a quick glance around, then scooted my hind end back inside the house, pushing Farley ahead of me, and grabbing Skunk as I ran. Skunk meowed in protest, but I kept him tucked firmly under my arm.

Mom ran in behind us and slammed the door. We hardly ever locked our house. If it wasn't safe out here in the back woods of Maine, where you knew everybody for miles around, then it wasn't safe anywhere.

Now, however, Mom locked the door. In fact, she double-locked it. She turned the little lock inside the door knob, and, higher up on the door, she also slid the dead bolt into place with a thunk.

"Stay right here," she ordered.

She ran to the rear of the house and locked the back door. Farley and I stayed in the kitchen, as she had instructed. I put my arm around his shoulder. We were too old to cower in a corner, cuddling each other, but still I wanted to touch my brother. This was a little scary.

Bruddy kind of pressed his face into my shoulder and held onto me.

Mom ran around the ground floor of the house, closing and locking the windows. She brushed her bangs out of her eyes as she ran from room to room. I could see she was trying to stay calm.

When all the doors and windows were locked, she paused, took a breath, and picked up the telephone.

"Sheriff Johnson, please," she said.

Chapter Seven

The sheriff arrived within fifteen minutes, with two deputies in tow.

His blue lights flashed and his siren screamed. I never realized until that moment how soothing the sound of a siren could be.

There wasn't much crime in Caldicott County — hardly any at all, in fact — and Sheriff Johnson aimed to keep it that way. A friend of mine who moved to Maine from New York City told me later that if you called the police in Manhattan and reported your tires slashed, they would laugh at you.

But Sheriff Johnson took this pretty seriously.

He was a thin, weather-beaten man with a face that looked like it was made out of old, well-worn leather. He looked tough, but kindly, too.

His deputies were both soft and pudgy — sort

of like the Pillsbury Dough Boy — and they didn't look too terribly smart.

Sheriff Johnson told my mother to keep us inside the house while he and his boys secured the area.

Farley and I watched with our noses pressed against the window. The deputies thrashed about in the woods for a while, looking to see if anyone was there and generally creating a commotion. Sheriff Johnson strung plastic yellow police tape across the entrance to the driveway.

It said, "Crime Scene — Do Not Cross."

Then he pulled on some rubber gloves, took what looked like a little paint brush, and started spreading powder all around the base of our car, on the tires themselves, and on the hubcaps.

I think he was dusting for fingerprints. I had read about it in books.

Sheriff Johnson walked slowly around the car, his eyes scanning the ground. Then he knelt down and looked under it, practically pressing one ear against the ground.

He stood up and walked toward the house.

"Do you have a baggie, ma'am?" he asked Mom.

"A baggie?"

"Yes, ma'am," he said. "A plastic sandwich bag, like?"

Mom gave him a baggie. He took it, walked back out to the car, knelt down, retrieved something from under the car, and plopped it into the baggie.

From the window, I couldn't see what it was, but I assumed it was some kind of evidence. I was happy he was working so diligently at solving our crime. I'd feel a lot more comfortable — a lot *safer*, actually — once they arrested someone and put him in jail. Whoever it was certainly deserved it, for scaring us like that.

Sheriff Johnson took the baggie back to his sheriff's car, which still had its blue lights flashing, then walked back to the house. He asked to speak to Mom in private.

"Sorry," he said to Farley and me. "Grown-up

stuff. I'm sure you understand." Then he winked at us.

I don't know why adults always think they have to exclude children when they're talking about important matters. Did he think we'd be scared to hear the truth?

I already *knew* some criminal had come right into our driveway and slashed our tires. I already knew there was some lunatic loose who might be dangerous.

But Bruddy and I dutifully left the kitchen. A little less dutifully, we stopped right outside the door and strained with all our might to overhear the conversation.

Sheriff Johnson had a low, rumbly voice, and it was hard for us to hear what he said. But we could hear Mom pretty well, and from her answers we could piece together the conversation pretty well.

"No, Sheriff," she said. "I can't imagine anyone who would want to do this. I just have no idea."

We heard the sheriff's voice rumbling unintelligibly again, then Mom replied in a tone of shock.

"Absolutely not," she said. "Bob and I had our differences, but he would never, ever do something like this. Never. Besides, he lives in Phoenix."

She was talking about Dad. I almost stamped my foot before I realized that the noise would be heard, and then the sheriff would realize we were eavesdropping. It made me mad for him even to suggest that Dad would do such a thing.

We heard his voice rumbling again, and Mom answering.

"A Swiss Army knife?" she asked. "Why, yes, Martin has one. Bob and I gave it to him for his birthday a couple of years ago. . . . Under the car? . . . Surely, Sheriff, you don't think Martin . . . "

Now, I was starting to get *really* steamed. First this dried up old boot of a sheriff was going to accuse my dad, and now he was going to suggest that *I* had done it!

I had hoped he was going to help us out. Now it was obvious that this shriveled old strap of a sheriff couldn't solve a crime even if the criminal walked right into his office and confessed.

I heard Mom calling my name. I went into the kitchen.

"Martin," she said, "could you show Sheriff Johnson your Swiss Army knife, please?"

"I'd be *glad* to," I said. I tried to keep my voice even, but I think a trace of anger might have crept into it.

I spun around, bounded up the stairs two at a time, and burst into my room. I strode over to my dresser. I'd show this sheriff character what an idiot he was.

I looked next to my squashed penny and my dollar bills, and froze. My heart stopped, and for a second I couldn't breathe.

My Swiss Army knife was gone.

Chapter Eight

Mom cried a lot.

Then she held me by both shoulders, looked me straight in the eye, and tearfully told me I had to tell her the truth. She had to know whether I had slashed the tires.

Sheriff Johnson had left, telling Mom he would call her later.

Mom and I were standing in the kitchen. Three full bags of beach stuff lay plopped on the floor where we had dropped them. I guessed we wouldn't be going to the beach that day, either.

I've already mentioned how much I hate to be accused of things I haven't done. It was happening yet again.

But I could see how upset Mom was, so I didn't stamp and shout and bolt up to my room and slam the door.

Instead, I looked her straight in the eye and told her the truth. I absolutely had not slashed the tires. I hadn't even thought of it.

And then I cried, too. I was kind of embarrassed about it. After all, I was twelve years old. Besides, Bruddy was watching the whole conversation from a polite distance, and I hated to cry in front of my little brother.

But I was really upset.

"Mom," I said, "I'm scared."

She looked at me with questioning eyes.

"I don't know if that was my knife Sheriff Johnson found under the car," I said. "But there is something I *do* know. Last night, before I went to sleep, I went around my room straightening everything up, you know? My CDs, my pencils, and all the stuff on top of my dresser?"

Mom looked at me and nodded.

"And, Mom," I said, my voice quavering and my eyes again starting to tear up. "My knife was in my room last night."

She stared at me without understanding.

"Mom, don't you see?" I said impatiently. "If it was there last night and it's missing today — and I didn't take it, which I didn't — someone *else* came into my room and took it!"

Mom's eyes darted to the kitchen door, where Farley was standing.

"No, Mom, honest," he said. "I didn't touch it."

Her eyes came back to me. She looked confused and frightened, and I did not like seeing my mother frightened. That did not quiet my fears one bit.

"Martin," she whispered. "Are you sure?"

I nodded, and the tears rolled down my cheeks.

Mom plucked a couple of tissues out of the box, honked into them a few times, and said she was going into her room to rest a while. Farley and I were not to go outside at all. We were to stay inside, with the doors and windows locked at all times.

Then she went into her room and closed the door.

Chapter Nine

Farley and I kicked around the house for a while, doing nothing in particular. Skunk wandered between our legs and around our feet, rubbing against us to try to get attention.

Usually, I gave Skunk all the attention he wanted, especially when I was feeling sad. Now I felt so depressed and hollow and scared that I just didn't have the energy.

The house, which usually struck me as bright and cheery, seemed dark and gloomy. Everything outside was gray. Rain streaked the windows. It splattered on the leaves and pounded the ground, falling in torrents and forming miniature rivers that ran down our driveway toward the road.

It was a good thing we hadn't gone to the beach. We wouldn't have had much fun anyway, getting caught in a storm like this.

Inside, it was so dark we almost had to turn on the lights. But not quite. Anyway, there wasn't anything we needed to see. We didn't feeling like playing Monopoly or anything. I was too upset even to read.

So Farley and I hung around in the kitchen, shrugging at each other, and not saying too much. Occasionally, both of us would stare at Mom's closed bedroom door.

She was supposed to comfort us at a time like this, I thought — calm us when we were nervous, soothe us when we were scared.

Dad would never just freak out and lock himself in his room.

I began to wish he were here. Moms weren't much good against eerie nighttime intruders, I decided.

The more I thought about someone coming into our house at night, while we were all asleep — and it had happened *twice* now, even if Mom didn't realize I hadn't eaten the peanut butter — the more frightened I became.

I thought maybe I would call Dad myself and ask him to come back to stay with us for a few days, just until this whole mess got straightened out. I asked Bruddy what he thought, but he just shrugged.

I decided to act. After all, Mom had told me I was the man of the house now. Sometimes, the man of the house had to be decisive.

I picked up the phone.

Before I could dial, I heard Mom's voice.

"Sheriff, I know my son," she was saying. "If he tells me he didn't do this, and that someone entered this house and took his knife, I believe him."

I held my fingers to my lips to shush Farley, who wasn't saying a word. I held the phone sideways, so he could listen, too.

In a low, rumbling voice dripping with sympathy, Sheriff Johnson suggested to Mom that teenage boys sometimes had certain phases they went through.

This made me mad. What the heck did that dried-up shoelace of a sheriff know? I wasn't even going to turn thirteen and become an official teenager for almost another year. Besides, the main thing was, *I hadn't done it!*

I got so angry I almost yelled into the phone. But I restrained myself.

Despite Mom's protests, the sheriff would not be persuaded. He kept talking about phases and growing pains. He suggested that Mom take me to a counselor, or ship me off to Phoenix to live with Dad if she was unable to handle me.

"Sheriff," Mom said, and there was a note of desperation in her voice. "This wasn't Martin who did this. We have an intruder on our hands, someone who is obviously very angry and dangerous. We need your help. We have got to have some protection."

"Ma'am, I'm sorry," Sheriff Johnson said. "There's nothing I can do."

Chapter Ten

Mom hung up and came out of her room into the kitchen.

Farley and I quickly pretended to be staring out the window at the rain. Farley even started to whistle, until I cracked him in the ribs with my elbow.

Mom's face was grim and white. She started cooking dinner, but she didn't say a word. Neither did we. Theoretically, I hadn't even heard her telephone conversation, so I couldn't very well tell her what I thought — which was that Sheriff Johnson was a stale strip of beef jerky with dog doo for brains.

Eventually, the silence got to be too much for me. The tension hung so heavily I could not stand the silence another minute. Without thinking, I began to whistle. Farley rammed his elbow into my waist.

We ate without saying too much besides, "Pass the peas." The whole meal was pretty uncomfortable.

Skunk meowed for his dinner. Mom got up, opened a can of cat food and fed it to him without cooing at him the way she usually did. Skunk looked up at her and meowed in a questioning way, almost as if he realized that something was wrong.

Then Mom sat back down, looked at her plate, and began rearranging the grains of rice with her fork. I didn't see her actually eat much of anything.

When we were done, Mom checked the locks on all the doors and windows for about the thirty-fifth time, then suggested that it was probably time for all of us to get some rest.

I could not go to sleep at all. I really tried. I lay still in my bed and tried all the tricks I knew. First I concentrated on relaxing my feet. Then I relaxed my knees. Then I relaxed my butt, and then my stomach, and my chest, and my arms, and my neck.

All that went pretty well. The problem came

when I tried to relax my brain. There was no way. I just couldn't do it.

I imagined fun things, like the time the whole family had gone hiking for five days in the White Mountains of New Hampshire, where all the peaks are named for presidents — Madison, Monroe, Washington, etc.

My dad said it was called the Presidential Range. I said that sounded like the stove in the White House kitchen.

Dad had laughed a lot. I liked it when I made Dad laugh.

Mom had just rolled her eyes and said, "Bob, why do you encourage him like that?"

I tried counting sheep leaping over a fence. I kept forgetting to keep counting, and five minutes later I would find myself worried stiff again, not thinking about leaping sheep at all.

The thing that had me worried was the intruder. Because there was no way around it. Not only had someone entered our house and eaten peanut butter. The intruder had actually crept up the stairs, eased open the door, and tiptoed right into my room.

While I was sleeping!

He'd been standing right over me while I snored peacefully, dreaming of Australian convicts getting beaten or starving at sea.

I felt as if my space had been violated. My room, which had been my refuge, my sanctuary, all my life, was no longer safe. If I couldn't be safe in my own room, then nothing in life was safe.

That was a very scary thought.

Scary, too, was the thought that the intruder might return. What he wanted, I could not fathom. Why had he taken my knife? To get me in trouble? To frame me for something I had not done?

What could be the reason for doing that? Did he know me? Did he have something against me?

And what would he do next?

I had no intention of finding out. I didn't want him to do anything next, besides go away.

I remembered that all the doors and windows

were locked, but still I did not feel safe. I got out of bed, pulled my chair out from behind my desk, and jammed it up under my doorknob.

I heard Skunk out in the hallway, so I moved the chair and opened the door to let him in.

I loved Skunk. He had just shown up at our house one day and moved in. It was the week after Dad moved out. I had been feeling kind of sad, because I hadn't realized yet that having your parents divorced wasn't all that bad.

Then this black and white cat just showed up out of nowhere. Almost as if he knew there was a vacancy in the house. As if he knew he was needed.

I named him Skunk because of his coloring, but he was really a sweet cat.

Now, I picked him up, carried him to my bed, and got in with him.

Then I read myself some soothing stories of Australian convicts escaping into the wild Australian outback, only to return a few weeks later with their eyes bulging, their ribs showing, and their bellies flat against their spines. They felt so hungry they were willing to endure any punishment just to get a little bit of nourishment.

I put the book down, switched off the light, and dozed off at last.

I was just getting into a really good dream about being a convict on a ship, and leading a mutiny because of insufficient rations, when something interrupted my sleep.

My eyelids fluttered open. It took me a second to realize I was in my room, not in the hold of a ship, and that it was nighttime, and that nothing was wrong.

My eyelids began to slide closed again.

This time I heard it.

Click.

Now my eyes were open wide. I sat bolt upright. Moonlight shone pale through the window. I looked around.

Nothing moved. Everything was in its place. No intruder loomed over me. The door was still closed, the chair still wedged under the doorknob.

My heart pounded like a drum. My pulse throbbed in my ears. Other than that, I heard nothing.

Calm down, I told myself. Use your eyes. Nothing is amiss. A pine needle must have blown against the window pane, I thought. Or perhaps a squirrel had dropped a nut onto our roof.

I took a deep breath and blew it out slowly, relaxing myself as best I could. I was about to slide under the covers when I heard the noise again.

Click.

My heart pounded louder than ever. If there had been another click, I don't think I could have heard it over the throbbing in my ears.

My eyes searched the darkness. A gleam across the room caught my gaze.

Slowly, slowly, shining in the moonlight, the doorknob began to turn.

Chapter Eleven

I sat frozen in horror.

I could feel my eyes bulging from their sockets. My mouth was open, trying to gasp for air. My chest strained and heaved, but I could not breathe. No air entered my lungs.

I started to panic. The intruder was coming in after me.

Absurdly, I told myself to be as quiet as possible. Maybe the intruder would hear nothing and go away.

I watched in frightened fascination. Slowly, the doorknob rotated in one direction. The door rattled a little. Then, just as slowly, the doorknob started turning the other way.

I tried to yell, "Mom!" But all that came out of my mouth was a hot, dry gust of air. I was too scared to make a sound.

The door began to rattle again. The intruder was pushing on it, trying to open it — wondering, no doubt, why it wouldn't swing open noiselessly the way it had the night before, when he had entered my room and stolen my knife.

The rattling grew louder, more vigorous, more forceful, more insistent. I didn't know what to do. I was so scared I started to tremble. The whole door was shaking.

I became convinced that whatever was out there was going to break down the door, splinter the chair, burst into the room and get me.

Finally, I gathered in a big chest full of air, found my voice, and yelled at the top of my lungs.

"LEAVE ME ALONE," I shouted. *"GO AWAY!"*

From the other side of the door, I heard a small voice.

"Martin, it's me," Farley said. "Let me in."

I let out the breath I had been holding for the last five minutes and ran to the door. I moved the chair, and let him in.

"I didn't mean to wake you up," he said apologetically. "I got a little frightened, thinking about everything that's happened and all. I just wanted to be near you."

I hugged him. It was probably the first time we'd hugged in a year. Boys don't hug much, you know.

"Come on," I said. "You can sleep with me tonight."

I jammed the chair back under the doorknob and we climbed into bed. Skunk stretched out across our feet. I noticed that he was getting pretty fat. The cat must like it here, I thought.

I felt more relaxed at once, even though Farley was just a little kid. I mean, what was he going to do if the intruder came in and attacked us. *I'd* have to protect *him*.

Still, right away I felt less scared. It was nice to have him near me. I yawned. Being terrified had tired me out. I felt my eyes start to close.

"Bruddy?" I said quietly.

"Huh?" he answered sleepily.

"When I shouted, 'Leave me alone, and go away?' "

"Yeah?"

"I thought the bad guy was there," I said. "That wasn't meant for you. I didn't mean for you to leave me alone and go away."

"I know that," he said, and fell asleep.

Chapter Twelve

I slept fitfully. I'm not used to sharing my bed with anyone. I woke up whenever Farley rolled over. Sometimes he'd yawn a great big yawn in his sleep, lazily reach across the bed, grab a fistful of covers, turn over — and yank every single blanket off me.

I think he even disturbed Skunk. After a while the cat, much as he liked us, gave up trying to sleep on the bed and went off to sleep on top of some shoes in my closet.

But I didn't mind. I was glad to have my Bruddy there with me.

The funny thing is that I woke up feeling more rested than I had in days. And happier.

Especially when we found out that nothing had

gone wrong in the middle of the night.

Believe me, we checked the house out thoroughly. Mom went through each room two or three times. Then she looked out the window at the car.

It was still sitting there on four flat tires. She had not had the time or the energy the day before to call someone to come replace them. But the car was otherwise undamaged.

Finally, Mom's face relaxed. The tight lines around the corners of her mouth eased, and she allowed herself a small smile. She even got a little color back into her cheeks.

Farley and I played cards. Skunk rubbed us for attention, and I held him in my lap while we played.

Mom called someone to come change all the tires. She had to repeat what she wanted several times, but finally a man in an olive-colored shirt and a greasy hat came out in a tow truck. He jacked up the car, one corner at time, changed all the tires, and presented Mom with a bill that just about made her faint.

"My first *car* didn't cost that much," she

grumbled to herself, but she wrote the man a check.

The sun shone brightly outside. It got hot and stuffy in the house, and Mom finally opened the windows. Fresh air poured in. Birds chirped. Chipmunks chattered.

It almost seemed as if we had imagined the terrible events of the day before. We knew that we had not. But it started to feel like maybe a traveling maniac had stopped by and attacked our car for no reason — and surely he was long gone and far away.

The sun sparkled so brightly and so happily it seemed nothing could possibly be wrong here. Probably, I thought, the intruder has gotten all the way to Nova Scotia by now.

The same thought even seemed to strike Mom.

"I don't want to jinx anything," she said with a half-smile. "But perhaps *tomorrow* we can go to the ocean."

After a while, she walked around the house, took a deep breath, and told us we could play outside if we wanted.

We went out behind the house and played store. I know, I know — I'm way too old to play pretend anything. But it was fun, just for one afternoon.

Bruddy and I went to a big boulder that stood taller than either one of us. It had natural ledges all around it that we used as shelves. We used acorns for merchandise, and leaves for cash.

We'd played that game a lot when we were younger. I guess it felt good to play the old game and remember the old times. Besides, we hadn't been together enough lately to develop many new things we liked to do together.

Mom called out that she was going to the supermarket, and she'd be back in an hour or so.

Farley and I gave up playing store and walked through the woods to the creek. The water babbled clear and cold over the smooth stones. The sun sparkled across the surface of the stream, dancing and playing and winking as the water ran and rippled.

Bruddy and I took our shoes off, rolled our pants up, sat on some stones, and dangled our feet into the cool waters. It felt terrific.

Chapter Thirteen

We actually talked that night at dinner. I mean, we actually said more than, "Pass the peas."

We talked about what fun it would be to go to the ocean in the morning. Mom said the weather forecast called for a beautiful day.

Of course, that had been the forecast the day before, and then our tires had been slashed and it had rained like the dickens. Rosy forecasts had a way of not turning out right. Just when you thought everything was going smoothly, you looked down and saw your best-laid plans circling the toilet bowl.

But there was nothing to do but hope for the best. Today, actually, had turned out better than I had thought it would. The sun had shone, the tires had been changed, and Mom had recovered.

She smiled at us.

"Did you boys have fun today?" she asked.

We nodded. Our mouths were full. Bruddy said something like "Mmmm, mmmmph," and then pointed at his stuffed cheeks to show why he couldn't speak clearly.

"It's so good to see you boys having a chance to spend time together again," Mom said.

"I can't wait for tomorrow," I said, swallowing a mouthful of mashed potatoes. "The last time we went to the ocean . . . "

I stopped. I had been about to talk about having a lot of fun with Dad. I didn't want to mention him and be the one responsible for making Mom sad.

"Uh . . . we had a really good time," I said.

"I remember," Mom said. Then she turned away and wiped at her eye with a knuckle. Maybe she just had a speck of dust in it. Then again, maybe I *had* made her sad.

Still, the whole family felt better. It seemed the

danger had passed. This whole episode with the tires and my knife being taken had been eerie, but it was over with. But, just in case, Mom still checked all the doors and windows to make sure they were locked.

That night, as I got ready for bed, I didn't feel nearly as scared as I had the night before. Nothing had happened to us. We were all safe, healthy and uninjured. Surely the intruder was miles away. Farley and I could each sleep in our own beds. Skunk could sleep at the foot of my bed undisturbed by Farley's thrashing.

But I did feel kind of down. I didn't know why. My heart just felt heavy in my chest. I scarcely even felt like reading.

I arranged all my stuff — my pencils, my CDs, my diary, my lucky penny. I picked up the picture of the four of us in the mountains — such a perfect family — and looked at it. It made me smile to remember it. I set the picture down exactly in its spot.

I had a hard time getting to sleep. I was mad at myself for having made Mom sad like that. Really, I had to be more careful. She was the best mom in the world, and she deserved to be happy. She didn't need some kid with a careless mouth making her feel unhappy all the time.

I decided I had to do better. It was my responsibility. After all, family members are supposed to make you feel good, not bad, right?

I read a little bit about how the convicts taken to Australia, if they screwed up again, were shipped to a little place called Norfolk Island. The punishment there was horrible, and the place was so isolated no one would ever know what was happening to you.

I turned out the light. There was no moon, only gloom. I wasn't frightened, exactly, the way I had been before. But I was possessed by a horrible feeling that something was going to go wrong, that the rosy forecast would go awry, that the things we counted on as a family were going to be wrecked.

A squirrel skittered on the roof. A branch blew against the window. And I was very sad.

Chapter Fourteen

I slept soundly, dreaming of floggings and starvation.

When I awoke, my gloom had lifted. I felt much better — relieved, almost.

I looked around. My room looked fine. I had certainly heard nothing strange going on in the night.

I started to make my bed. I thought about the ocean. Good thing our beach bags were still packed — as they had been for two days. I felt happy.

At least I did until I heard my mother yelling downstairs.

"*Mar*-tin! Please!" she hollered. "Come down here this minute!"

I wondered what in the world could be wrong

now. I padded barefoot down the stairs.

The kitchen was a mess. The new jar of peanut butter Mom had just bought at the grocery store lay empty on the floor. A sticky spoon lay beside it. Peanut butter was spread everywhere — on the faucets, in the sink, on the counter.

Jelly was plopped across the floor.

I looked up at Mom. Her face was as white as new-fallen snow in a Maine winter.

"Martin, why?" she asked.

I shook my head.

"No, Mom . . ." I started to say.

She just stared at me white-faced and pointed at the other side of the room. The peanut butter and jelly was not the worst of it.

Our breakfast table and the four chairs around it were smashed.

I gaped. It was impossible to understand. There were hardly any pieces big enough to recognize as furniture. The floor was littered with splinters the size of match sticks.

It was amazing that we had slept through it. We must have been exhausted from the worry of the last couple of days. Then, when we had thought at last we were safe, we had slept as soundly as bears in hibernation.

I looked over at Mom. Her lower lip trembled, and I thought she was about to cry.

"Martin, why?" she whispered.

"Mom, I swear . . . " I said.

"Martin, all the doors and windows were locked."

"But Mom, surely you don't think that I . . . "

Suddenly, Farley yelled.

"Oh! Mom! Mom! Martin!" he screamed. "Look at this! Look! Look!"

I raced over to see what he was pointing at. Mom walked over slowly, trying to dodge the peanut butter and jelly plopped all over the floor. Farley was on his knees, examining something on the floor.

In the midst of a huge blob of jelly, there was a footprint. An animal footprint. A *huge* animal footprint.

It looked like one of Skunk's paw-prints, except for two things. First, you could see where the toenails had been, and cats walk with their toenails retracted. Second, this paw-print was as big as a good-sized pancake.

Mom and I stood looking with our mouths hanging open.

"And look at this," Farley said.

He pulled from the jelly a clump of brown fur. It wasn't Skunk's, because all his fur was black and white. I have brown hair, but this was fur — definitely not human.

Mom made a little croaking noise in her throat. Then she put both hands to her lips, said, "Oh, my heavenly days," walked away about three steps, and fainted. Right in the middle of all that peanut butter and jelly.

Her head hit the floor hard.

Chapter Fifteen

For a moment, Farley and I stood stock still. We had no idea what to do.

Farley grabbed a dish towel and began waving it vigorously over Mom's face, trying to fan her back to consciousness. Then he started to fill a pitcher of water, but when I realized that he meant to pour the whole thing over Mom's head, I made him stop.

I was plenty worried. If you've never seen your mom unconscious on the floor, you probably wouldn't understand. It is very unsettling. When your parent is out cold, you feel like you're the one responsible for everything.

I tried to keep as calm as I could. I ran to get a pillow to put under Mom's head. Then I remembered that I'd read somewhere that fainting comes from lack of blood in the brain, and the best thing to do is to elevate the victim's legs. That way the blood can run downhill out of the legs and be more accessible to the brain. So I got two more pillows and put them under Mom's feet.

Farley was getting upset, jumping in place, flapping his hands around, and saying, "Oh! Oh! Oh!" I didn't find that particularly helpful.

I decided he was getting upset because he had nothing to do that would make him feel useful.

"Quick," I said. "We've got to check the house to make sure that whatever made that footprint isn't still inside. And check all the windows, too. You do the upstairs. I'll look down here."

Farley looked grateful for an assignment, but he seemed nervous about the idea that the *thing*, for lack of a better word, might still be in the house. He looked at first as if he was going to bound up the stairs. Then he thought better of it, and tiptoed up them one by one.

As quickly as I could, I checked the downstairs — Mom's bedroom, the dining room, and the living room. I had thought I would run through the house checking each room quickly, because Mom needed help. But I wound up being a lot more cautious than that.

Each time I got to a new room, instead of running right into it, I sort of poked my eyeballs around the doorway first, just to check things out.

I really did not want to see whatever had made that huge paw print in the jelly and smashed our kitchen furniture to smithereens. More importantly, I did not want *it* to see *me*.

As I got ready to peer into the living room, I heard a loud clunk. Quickly, I flattened myself against the wall next to the doorway, trying to melt into the wallpaper. I held my breath.

I heard nothing but the pounding of my heart. My ears throbbed with the booming of my own heart-beat. I held my breath.

I felt certain that whatever was in the living

room would soon lumber through the doorway, spot me, and attack.

I decided I didn't want to see death coming. I closed my eyes.

Chapter Sixteen

I held my breath and kept my eyes closed for what seemed like forever.

I could hear Farley tromping about upstairs. I wanted to yell out to him, to warn him not to come downstairs, to jump out a window and flee while he still had a chance.

But if I yelled, the beast or whatever it was would hear me. And that would be the end of me. Certain death.

So I kept quiet, holding my breath and feeling that I wasn't a very good brother after all. It was my responsibility to warn him, no matter how great the risk. A braver kid would have warned *his* brother, to protect him from harm.

I heard Farley start to descend the stairs. He was coming down, step by step by step, unaware of the danger that awaited him downstairs. And I said nothing, not daring to speak, hoping against hope that somehow things would work out all right even if I wasn't doing the right thing.

After that first big clunk, I heard no more noise from the living room. Slowly, I took a breath and opened my eyes — just in time to see Skunk stroll lazily out of the living room, right past where I stood plastered against the wall, frozen in fright.

All the air whooshed out of me like a balloon. Was *that* all I had heard? A cat jumping off the couch?

I poked my eyeballs around the doorway and took a look. A vase lay knocked over on the coffee table. Skunk had knocked it over a million times before.

I was relieved, but I also wanted to drop kick that cat about a hundred yards into the end zone. Scaring me like that — it made me mad.

Just then, Farley came around the corner.

"Nothing upstairs," he announced, then stopped. "What's the matter?" he asked. "You look like you've seen a ghost."

"Naw," I said. "A cat."

He looked at me like there was something wrong with me, but I had no time to explain. Mom still lay unconscious on the kitchen floor.

And we still had a very big problem at this house. Bigger than ever, once I stopped to think about it.

Because if locked windows and doors had not managed to keep out whatever kind of beast was trying to get at us, then our house — which for my whole life had been my place of safety, my refuge — was not safe at all.

Chapter Seventeen

Mom was regaining consciousness by the time we got back to the kitchen.

Her eyelids fluttered like the wings of a butterfly. She moaned a couple of times, then opened her eyes, sat up and put her hand to her forehead.

She looked around. Her eyes started to roll back into her head, and for a minute I thought she was going to faint again. But she didn't. Instead, she got slowly to her feet and wobbled off toward her bedroom.

"Kids, I need to lie down for a while," she said.

It occurred to me that she had just *been* lying down for a while, but I didn't point that out. I also didn't point out that, unless she got out of those clothes, she was going to get peanut butter and jelly all over her sheets.

I was worried about her. And a little mad at her. We were in danger, and instead of protecting us, she was going to bed. Fat lot of good that would do!

I wished Dad were here. He'd protect us. Actually, it occurred to me that I should call him and let him know what was going on. Maybe he would drop everything to come out and save us.

But, as Mom tottered into her bedroom, she paused at her doorway, and looked back at me.

"Please call Sheriff Johnson," she said. "Tell him we don't feel that we're safe here."

Then she shut the door behind her.

I called the miserable old strip of leather. I told him everything that had gone on — how the food had been spread around, and the furniture had been smashed, and the intruder had somehow gotten into the house even though all the doors and windows were locked. I told him about the huge animal footprint in the jelly, and the clump of fur that Farley had found.

He listened to it all in silence. Then he asked to speak to Mom.

"I'm sorry," I said. "This whole thing has scared her so badly she's gone to bed. She can't come to the phone right now."

"Son," Sheriff Johnson said, "I am trying as hard as I can to be patient with you. I know you may be going through some tough times right now. But first you committed an act of vandalism, when you slashed your mother's tires. Now you're filing a false report with authorities. Both of those are crimes, son. Please don't push me any further."

"But sheriff!" I practically yelled into the phone. "I'm telling the truth! You need to help us! We're not safe!"

"Good-bye, son," the sheriff said, and hung up.

I looked at Mom's closed door, then over at Farley. We were in grave danger. And we were completely on our own.

Chapter Eighteen

Night fell, and still Mom slept in her room.

I could not think of how we could protect ourselves. We had already locked all the doors and windows, and that had not helped one bit. Could whatever strange beast was after us pass right through walls, like a ghost? If not, how had it gotten inside our house?

I climbed up to bed with a heavy heart. I saw Farley into bed — and told him to brush his teeth — because Mom had not gotten up yet. Then I went into my room, braced my chair under the doorknob, changed into my pajamas, climbed into bed, and started to read.

I read about how the rich snooty people in

Australia didn't like even the children of criminals, and wanted them to remain second-class citizens forever. It was as if the children were somehow to blame for what the parents had done. That didn't seem fair to me.

Surprisingly, I drifted off to sleep quite quickly. I guess I was just flat-out exhausted from what had happened that day.

I slept deeply, as still as a log on the forest floor, undisturbed by anything.

Until suddenly I was roused by the sound of frantic yelling, and a furious pounding on my door.

I heard Farley screaming hysterically.

"Mom! Mom! Mom! Mom!" he yelled at the top of his lungs. "Help! Help! Help!"

The hammering on my door continued, nearly deafening me.

From further away, probably at the bottom of the stairs, I heard Mom yelling hoarsely, "What? What? What? What?" She sounded very frightened.

"Mom! Mom!" Farley yelled.

It was still dark, not yet dawn. I leapt out of bed to see what was going on. But as I stood up, a terrible pain in my side doubled me over. I sank to my knees and leaned forward until the top of my head touched the floor. I hugged my rib cage. The pain was so intense I thought I might throw up.

The yelling and banging outside continued. Mom's voice was closer now, and she was calling my name. My side hurt so badly I could barely hear her.

I sat back up and lifted my pajama top. On the left side of my chest, I saw a deep purple welt. It seemed to swell even as I looked at it. I touched it and gasped. The bruise was deep.

I managed to get to my feet. My head spun and I reeled toward the doorway. I heard Mom right outside now. She and Farley were both screaming my name and pounding. The door was practically jumping off its hinges.

I moved the chair from under the doorknob, and the door almost flew into my face from their hammering. Mom and Farley burst into the room and looked frantically around everywhere — in the closet, behind the door, under the bed — before turning back to me.

"Oh, Martin!" Mom yelled, and hugged me so tightly my bruise felt like a stab wound. "Thank goodness you're all right!"

She started crying onto my shoulder. Farley cried and held tightly to my hand.

I could not figure out what had happened. Then Farley, sniffling and shaking, told me he had been woken up by a noise in the upstairs hallway outside our rooms.

"I looked out the door of my room," he said, hiccuping and trying not to cry. "And I saw the *thing!*"

"What thing?" I asked, pulling away from Mom and holding my side again.

"The *beast!*" Farley said. "It was huge and hairy and snarling, and it had big teeth, and it was heading right toward your room!"

The hair on the back of my neck stood up.

"Then what?" I whispered.

"I wanted to stop it!" Farley said, and he started crying again. "I tried, Martin. Honest I tried."

"What then?" I croaked.

"I ran into my room and got my baseball bat and I ran out and I whacked it hard in the stomach," Farley said. "But it just threw me aside and went into your room and slammed the door behind it. That's when I started yelling for Mom. I'm sorry. I tried my hardest to stop it."

Every nerve in my body tingled with fear. The beast had broken into my room and attacked me, viciously — and *that* was the reason I felt such a terrible pain in my side. Slowly, I looked around my room.

There was no beast. Everything seemed to be in its place. My slippers were lined up neatly beside my bed. My diary and my pencils were lined up perfectly.

Then my eyes scanned the dresser top.

The picture! My favorite picture — the one of the whole family together and happy, was ruined. The beast had smashed the frame, broken the glass into a thousand shards, ripped the picture into tiny bits, and hurled the pieces all over the room.

I started to cry. I had loved that picture. Now I would never see it again.

Chapter Nineteen

"Where'd he go, that beast?" Farley asked, quaking. "Is he coming back?"

"I don't know, and I hope not," I replied. "First of all, if he can get *in* the house with all the doors and windows locked, he probably doesn't need the door opened for him on his way out."

Farley wanted to know then whether the beast was some kind of spirit or ghost. I shrugged. I had no idea what it was.

I only knew one thing. Whatever it was, it was very angry. And for reasons I could not explain, it seemed to be angriest at me.

I mean, the thing had practically framed me for the peanut butter job. Then it had *definitely* framed me for the tire-slashing incident, by stealing my knife and planting it under the car.

Now, its anger was growing. It wasn't content any more with trying to get me in trouble with my mother, or with Sheriff Johnson. Now the thing had barged into my room, destroyed the thing I held most precious, and attacked me physically.

Mom examined my bruised chest again. My side was really starting to turn black and blue.

She told me and Farley to come down to her room. First, I looked around my room for Skunk, but he was missing. That worried me.

Down in her room, Mom switched on all the lights, and took care of me. She wrapped some ice cubes in a paper towel and had me press it against the bruise. She gave me a couple of aspirin, too, and announced we would all sleep together in her bed for the rest of the night.

I was scared stiff, now that I realized I was the primary target of the beast's anger. But I'll say this for Mom. Now that things were really dangerous, she was fairly calm. She didn't cry or faint. She took care of us. She did her best to defend the family.

Before we all piled into her bed, she told us she was sorry, but we needed to wait by ourselves in her room for just one minute. Then she grabbed the flashlight and went outside in her nightgown, leaving Farley and me alone and scared, even though all the lights were on.

She returned in no time, carrying the ax from our woodshed.

This she placed under the bed. She thought about it for a minute, then went to the kitchen and came back with two huge carving knives. She put them under the bed with the ax.

"I don't think whatever it is will bother us now," she said in as light a tone as she could muster.

I felt very uneasy. I had the awful feeling that something terrible was about to happen.

Farley got into bed on one side of Mom. Fearfully, I climbed into bed on the other side. For some reason, I did not feel as if I ought to be there.

Suddenly, I realized what it was.

If the beast was after me, and I slept in the same bed with them, I was putting the whole family in danger. The angry thing could come in looking for me, start smashing everything in the bed, and Farley and Mom would be hurt.

All because of me.

"Mom," I said quietly into the darkness. "Are you sure you want me here? Because if that thing is after *me*, then . . . "

My voice trailed off.

Mom leaned over, kissed me, and put her arm across my chest.

"Yes, sweetheart," she said. "I'm very sure I want you here."

Chapter Twenty

Comforted by my mother's warmth, I soon fell asleep.

When I awoke, it was still dark. I'm not sure what woke me up. I think maybe I had to go to the bathroom. As I lay in the bed deciding whether or not to get up, I felt very strange.

Somehow, I felt oddly angry at everything that was going on. I felt mad that we were being frightened like this, so that we each couldn't sleep comfortably in our own beds. I felt angry that Dad wasn't there to protect us, but was instead snoozing peacefully in Phoenix, blissfully unaware that anything was wrong. And I felt furious that we were under attack.

More than anything, I wanted to get my hands

on the beast that was threatening my family. I felt so mad I wanted to tear him limb from limb.

Quietly, I swung my feet over the edge of the bed and sat up. I was confused for a minute. Then I remembered — all I needed was to go to the bathroom and then go back to sleep. A bad dream must have made me feel this way.

Still, the strange and angry feeling persisted.

I stood up and felt my way along the wall towards Mom's bathroom. I'm so familiar with my own room that I can get around it in the pitch black without bumping into things. I know exactly how many steps it is from the desk to the dresser, or from the door to my bed.

But I wasn't used to Mom's room. Of course, I had been mostly banned from it when Mom and Dad were still married. This was their private place, and I was not allowed in without knocking — and rarely was allowed in at all.

So I wasn't that familiar with how it was laid out, and how to get where I was going in the pitch dark without slamming into something and waking everybody up.

But I had to get to the bathroom.

I tried to picture the room as I groped around the walls with my hands. Ah, here was Mom's dressing table. Then back to the wall. And this was . . . Mom's dresser. Just a little further along the wall, and I should come to the bathroom door. Yes, here it was . . .

I slid inside the bathroom and closed the door quietly in the darkness. I didn't want to wake up Mom and Farley by turning on the light with the bathroom door open.

With the door safely closed, I flicked on the light, and winced at the sudden brightness.

I walked over to the toilet, lifted the lid, and sat down. I learned a while ago never to go the bathroom standing up when I'm half-asleep. And I was half-asleep. As I sat on the toilet, my head would suddenly droop forward as I nodded off. Then I would feel the surge of anger rising, and I would lift my head, and it felt like my eyes would almost roll back into my skull.

Something was wrong with me. Something was very wrong.

Red-hot rage rose inside me until I thought it would burst forth in a roar.

I flushed the toilet and walked over to the counter.

Slowly, almost unwilling, I raised my eyes to the mirror. And there it was, looking back at me, ferocious and angry and frothing — and ready to attack.

I screamed as loud as I could.

Chapter Twenty-One

I had never been so terrified in my life. I had never put so much effort into a scream before.

But no scream came out. Nor anything like a scream. The only sound I made was a long, low growling noise from far back in my throat, like the yawn of a lion.

I had never felt so alone, so isolated, so frightened. But when I gazed into the mirror, I did not see the face of a scared, lonely twelve-year-old boy.

I saw looking back at me the hairy, angry face of a beast.

Foot-long fur hung off my cheeks and forehead and chin. My eyes were bloodshot, and they rolled crazily in their sockets. My teeth were big and gleaming and snarling.

I looked down at my hands. They were covered with hair. Claws stuck out where my fingernails had been.

In a horrible, chilling moment, I realized it all. The beast that had been trying to destroy our family was me.

A strange, horrible mix of emotions rushed over me. I felt ravenously hungry, desperate for any kind of nourishment. I felt furious at everything — at all the bad luck, and the divorce, and the broken plate, and at the terrible spell that had been cast over me, turning me into a marauding beast that went into happy homes and destroyed them at night while no one was looking.

Rage burned within me. I felt as if I was out of all control. There was no telling what I would do next, who I would hurt, what I would destroy.

The next minute, I felt more frightened than ever. Mom and Farley were sleeping quietly in the next room. If they woke up and saw me in this condition, they would grab their weapons and . . .

. . . And kill me.

They would hack my head off with the ax, or plunge a knife deep into my heart, again and again and again. Who could blame them?

Anyone would want to kill the beast that was destroying his family.

Then an even more horrible thought swept over me like a wave, numbing my anger for a moment. I reeled against the wall and held my head in my hairy hands.

I was the raging beast. They were sleeping peacefully not twenty feet away.

I had to get out of the house. I had to flee. Unless I ran for all I was worth and got as far away from here as I could, then possibly, maybe . . .

. . . I would kill them.

Chapter Twenty-Two

I needed to get out, to get as far away from the people I loved as I could.

I tiptoed toward the bathroom door, my toe-claws clacking against the tile floor. I put one hairy paw on the doorknob, and flicked the lights off with the other.

Silently, I turned the knob and eased the bath-room door open. The last thing I wanted to do was wake up Mom and Farley. I didn't want them to come after me with their weapons, and I didn't want to find myself going after them, either.

I crept out of the bedroom, walked softly across the kitchen, and stopped at the door. Quietly, I rotated the lock in the doorknob. I reached up and, ever so slowly, slid the dead bolt open.

Holding my breath, I opened the door inch by inch, praying the hinges would not squeak. When it was open about a foot, I squeezed through, quietly closed the door behind me, and started feeling my way across the yard in the darkness.

I stopped and turned around. Maybe I should have locked the door behind me, I thought, to keep Mom and Farley safe.

Then, with anger and hatred rising like vomit in my throat, I realized there was no need. The only danger they faced was me.

I turned again and started running through the woods. No moon shone. The night was blacker than coal. I could see nothing.

Tree branches scratched my cheeks and lashed my eyes, but I didn't care. I tripped and fell sprawling and snarling on the ground. Angrily, I scrambled up and ran on, thrashing my way through the forest, roaring as I went.

I had no idea which way I was going. I had no

destination in mind. Probably there was no place for people like me, under the terrible spell of an anger that transformed them into something dangerous and unrecognizable.

I only needed to get away, far, far away, where I could not hurt anyone any more.

I do not know how far I ran. I thundered on and on, getting madder and madder, knocking bushes and saplings out of my way with my claws.

Rage overwhelmed me. I stopped and snapped a branch off a tree and began beating everything around me — bushes, trees, stones, whatever — until the branch had splintered in my hands.

I went stark raving mad. I thrashed about, ripping vines out of the ground and kicking stones, roaring and snorting, beating tree trunks with my fists.

I stopped for a moment to catch my breath, heaving and panting. The first light of day was beginning to filter through the leaves. Dawn was breaking.

I staggered a few steps, confused and spent, and dropped in a heap on the bank of a stream. As the water babbled and laughed over the stones beside me, I curled into a ball and wept.

Chapter Twenty-Three

I do not know how long I slept.

The sun was high in the sky when I awoke, so perhaps it was midday. I didn't really care. I had no place to go, nowhere I wanted to be.

I was desperately hungry, though. I needed food like a baby needs its mother's milk. I rose up, determined to do anything necessary to get the sweet comfort of food in my belly.

I struggled to my feet. I was so hungry I became disoriented. Food seemed so important to me that it was more than just food — it was caring, it was love, it was life itself. I had to have some now, at all costs.

But how? Where?

All I could think of was the fresh groceries, the new jars of peanut butter and jelly at my mother's house. I would have to break in — I didn't consider it my house any more — and steal that food and gorge myself until my stomach was heavy and full.

Then the gnawing, empty feeling would finally leave me. I would feel warm and comfortable and fulfilled, like the baby who finally turns its face away from the bottle, sleepy and satisfied and loved.

I wasn't sure where I was. I thought this might be the same stream in which Farley and I had dangled our feet, only perhaps I was further downstream. If I followed it upstream, nearer its source, maybe I would find the way back home.

I bent over the sparkling waters and looked at my reflection. The horrible face of the beast stared back at me. I winced and drew back.

I started to walk alongside the stream. I took only two steps before I heard voices in the woods.

"He's on the move, Sheriff!" a man's voice called.

"I see him. Head around that way and cut him off," replied a voice I recognized as belonging to that miserable old bootstrap of a sheriff.

I looked ahead. The two Pillsbury Dough Boy deputies were ahead of me, one on either side of the stream. They held their billy clubs at the ready.

I looked the other way, downstream. Two men I did not recognize stood there, slapping their night-sticks into the palms of their hands.

On my right I saw two more men approaching through thc brush. Across the stream, I saw two more.

I was trapped. The anger welled up inside me again. I drew myself up to my full, bear-like height, threw my head back, and roared with rage.

I looked around again. All the men had pistols strapped to their hips. As I looked at one of the dough boys, I saw him unsnap the strap that held his gun in his holster. His eyes were wide. His chins were trem-bling.

I realized that to them I was a fearsome, hor-rible beast, dangerous and menacing. And that, likely as not, they were going to draw their guns and shoot. There would be a blaze of gunfire from all sides, and I would jerk and twitch my way through the forest until I fell to the ground with blood oozing from a dozen bullet holes.

I tried to talk, to tell them it was really me, Martin. They shouldn't be scared, and they shouldn't shoot.

But I could not form words. The only sound that escaped my mouth was an angry growl. There was no way to tell them.

The other dough boy unstrapped his holster, too. I looked around in despair. These men were going to kill me. And they were going to do it without ever knowing who I really was.

Chapter Twenty-Four

I had only one chance, and that was to run. I needed to run as I had never run before. I had to run for my life.

My powers of reasoning were dimmed, I knew, but I decided to run upstream to try to get past the doughboys. I figured they must be pretty slow.

I lowered my head and charged. The woods and the stream and the men merged into one indistinct blur. Whipping by my head I saw colors but no shapes. The men erupted into a symphony of shouts, their frantic yells filling the forest with clamor.

"Get him! . . . There! . . . This way! . . . No! No! Don't let him head off that way!"

Colors streaked by my face. I saw outstretched

arms trying to block my path. I turned, and the green of the leaves whirred before my eyes again.

The men shouted and called, some of them screaming, others barking orders, some voices high, others low.

"Get him! Get him! Get him! . . . No! The other way! . . . Get the net! Get the net! . . . Come on, over him, over him! Get it over the top of him! . . . Ahhhh! . . . That's it, that's it!"

On all sides, a heavy rope net closed in on me. I fought it with my arms, but they became entangled. I kicked and caught my legs in the net and fell heavily on my back.

"OK! . . . You got him! . . . Now stand clear!"

I struggled and wrestled and writhed. The net only closed more tightly around me. Finally, I could struggle no more. I lay there panting, at their mercy.

Gradually, the men approached. I heard their footsteps near my head, and saw their boots near my face. They stood all around me, talking amongst themselves.

I snorted and looked at them wildly.

Sheriff Johnson knelt down beside me and peered into my face.

"Worst case I've ever seen," he said. "Of course, I've only seen two others. But this is the worst."

"What is it, Sheriff?" another voice asked.

"The scientific term is Cholera Metamorphosis," the sheriff said slowly. "It's a form of anger so extreme, it is actually physically disfiguring. The victim is transformed by rage into an entirely different kind of being."

The sheriff squinted at me and chewed thoughtfully on a sprig of grass. I glared up at him, breathed heavily, and struggled briefly with the net.

"Transformed, actually, into an animal," thc sheriff continued.

"Sheriff, can anything be done?" asked my father's voice.

My father? *He* was here? He'd arrived just a little too stinking late, if you wanted my opinion. He was like the cavalry charging in after the battle had been forever lost.

I became more furious than ever. I roared and bucked and struggled until my muscles burned and I could struggle no more.

My father had traveled all the way from Phoenix, and he had to see me like this.

I gasped for air, and could not seem to get enough. The sky whirled and the voices around me grew faint. I could barely hear them.

"The cure is very difficult, sir," I heard the sheriff say. "And the victim has to do it for himself. No one else can do it for him."

Chapter Twenty-Five

Some hours must have past. I think I slept. The men talked to each other.

I heard a pickup leave with a slamming of doors and a spinning of wheels. I slept again and, later, I heard it return. The doors slammed, the tailgate clanged open, and a bunch of men called, "Easy, now," to each other.

I could not see, but it sounded as if they were lifting something bulky and fragile out of the back of the pickup, taking care to lift it evenly at all corners and not to drop it. Then, from the grunts and the groans and the scraping, it sounded as if they were unloading something extremely heavy.

I struggled briefly, gave up, and lay there,

sometimes dozing, sometimes awake. The men marched around, taking no notice of me, their boots passing within inches of my face.

The sky swirled and the trees whirled and the voices grew faint.

I thought I heard my father trying to hurry the men along. I thought I heard my mother crying, and my father trying to comfort her.

The sheriff bent down near my face again.

"Son, can you hear me?" he said.

I nodded and made a sound that was somewhere between a snort and a sob.

"We're gonna let you out of this net," he said. "But you gotta promise to do everything exactly as we say."

I said nothing. I could hardly hear him.

The sheriff put a hand on my shoulder and bent even closer to me.

"We can help you, son," he said. He was speaking loudly right into my face. My eyes rolled in their sockets, fixed on his face, and tried to focus.

"We're gonna turn you loose from this net, but you gotta promise to do everything exactly as we say. Have we got a deal?"

I was exhausted. Slowly I nodded my head. I tried to speak, but all that emerged from my mouth was a low moan.

Several of the men lifted me upright. My arms were still pinioned, and I could not have gotten up by myself.

Sheriff Johnson stood right in front of me. His two doughy deputies stood behind him, further back, fear showing in their eyes. I wanted to tell them, no, don't be afraid, it's only me, Martin, trapped in here.

I wanted to cry.

The sheriff looked me right in the eye, and spoke to me very softly.

"We got a deal, right?" he asked.

Again, I nodded.

With the help of his deputies, Sheriff Johnson began unfastening the net. The deputies reached in toward the net with their hands, but leaned away with their bodies, ready at any moment to run for their lives.

Finally, the net was undone. It fell harmlessly at my feet. Step by step, the sheriff and his deputies backed away from me.

"You have to do this for yourself," the sheriff called. "You have to do this for yourself."

The forest seemed suddenly eerie. The black trunks of the trees stretched high overhead until their branches met like the roof of a cathedral. Shafts of sunlight sliced down between the dark trunks.

I stood in the midst of a covered clearing. Light glowed between the trees, but the clearing was dim.

Suddenly, I was startled by the sound of an organ. The high, clear notes pierced the quiet like the gleaming steel of a sword.

I looked to the edge of the clearing. My mother, tears streaming down her face, sat at an organ, playing. This must have been something brought in on the truck, I thought. The heavy thing, no doubt.

•

My mother looked at me. She was dressed all in white. The sunlight blurred her image, wrapping her in a gauzy glow.

The notes cut into my soul. I felt sad and frightened and trapped and alone.

"Walk forward, son." It was Sheriff Johnson's voice. "Now pick up that club."

On the ground I saw a large wooden club, like an overgrown baseball bat, or something a caveman would wield. I looked questioningly at the Sheriff. His deputies stood nearby, their nightsticks at the ready.

"Go on," Sheriff Johnson called. "Pick it up."

I stooped and grasped the club in my right hand.

"Now look up," the sheriff commanded.

I gazed across the clearing. Standing on the other side, also carrying a club, was the most monstrously ugly, hideously deformed beast I have ever seen.

It reared up at the sight of me. I looked over at Sheriff Johnson.

"Go get it, son," he called. "This is a fight to the death. You have to kill it!"

Chapter Twenty-Six

I shook my head. No matter how hideous the beast was, I could not kill it.

I started to put the club down and back away, but again the sheriff called to me.

"You promised me, son," he said. "You've got to do it! You have to!"

I hesitated. I heard my father's voice.

"Martin, you can do it. You can do it. Please!"

Still, my mother played the organ. The haunting notes echoed through the tall clearing, heartbreaking and inspiring.

I walked toward the beast. He began to walk toward me. Our eyes locked. Neither of us would look away.

My heart pounded in my chest. I wasn't a fighter! What if he killed me instead of me killing him?

Every move I made, he challenged. If I advanced on him, he advanced on me. If I raised my club, he raised his. If I circled to my right, he circled to his left to cut me off.

It was as if he was mimicking me, mocking me, making fun.

I felt my anger start to rise. I took three deep breaths, preparing to charge. The music played. Everything suddenly seemed sharply clear — the outlines of the leaves, the bark on the tree trunks, the shadows on the forest floor.

I could even see the color of the other beast's eyes — hazel, like my own. They looked angry and sad and frightened and threatening and bloodshot.

My mother played. My father called encouragement.

Slowly, I advanced on my enemy. Step by step, we drew closer. I knew what I had to do. It was clear to me now.

Suddenly, I raised the club over my head, roared, and charged. In a frenzy, I attacked. Over and over, I swung the club, furiously raining blows onto the beast, beating him without mercy.

Until there was nothing left but shards of glass on the ground.

Chapter Twenty-Seven

Quickly, I realized the other beast had been nothing but a huge mirror placed across the clearing.

The ugly, deformed beast had been me.

I looked up. Another mirror stood behind the one I had smashed. Reflected back at me, I saw the frightened, tear-stained face of a twelve-year-old boy.

Someone grabbed me roughly from behind, grabbing a hank of my hair and forcing me to look into the mirror.

It was my father, shouting wildly into my ear.

"Do you like getting blamed for things you haven't done?" he bellowed. "Do you? Do you?"

"No!" I screamed. "I hate it! I hate it!"

"Is it fair when somebody does that to you?"

my father yelled. "Is it fair, huh?"

"It's not fair!" I screamed. "It's not fair!"

My father thrust my face at the mirror.

"Then stop doing it to that kid in the mirror!" he yelled. "Stop blaming him for things he had nothing to do with!"

"But I did it!" I wailed. "I wrecked everything! I drove your car over Mom's bike, and all the other bad things, and if it weren't for me, you'd still be married! I did it! I did it!"

"No! No! No! No!" my father bellowed. "You had nothing to do with it! Nothing! Stop blaming that kid in the mirror for things he hasn't done! Stop it! Stop it!"

"It's not my fault!" I yelled. "It's not my fault! It's not my fault!"

My father relaxed his grip on my hair. I turned around and hugged him and sobbed into his shoulder.

"It's not my fault," I said.

"No," he said softly. "It's not your fault. None of it is. Not even one little bit."

Chapter Twenty-Eight

Dad stayed around for a few days after that, while I recuperated, though he slept on the couch. Mom cried over me a lot and said she was sorry. Sheriff Johnson would occasionally stop by, tip his hat to me, and tell me he hoped I was feeling fine.

I was feeling relieved, as much as anything. For one thing, I realized now that my family had never really been in danger. The beast had not been mad at them — not really.

The beast had been angry at me. I had been mad at myself, furiously, hideously angry, because I thought I had caused my parents' divorce. And I had set out to punish myself. I made other people mad at me, first Mom and then the sheriff. Then I had punished myself more by destroying the possessions I prized.

The bruise on my side had been Farley — that brave, wonderful brother of mine — hitting the beast with a baseball bat while trying to protect me. Only, I *was* the beast.

I spent a few days in bed, because the whole ordeal had been exhausting. Mom and Dad came into my room together and sat down and told me their divorce had nothing to do with me. There had been things they couldn't agree on, and those things were not related to me at all.

They said they were mad at themselves for letting me think I was to blame. I told them it was OK for them to be mad at themselves — but only a little bit. I didn't want *them* turning into beasts, too.

Just one thing preyed on my mind. Skunk was still missing. I was afraid that, to punish myself even further, I had killed my pet, the animal that had come to comfort me in my time of need.

Farley spent a lot of time in my room, playing

cards and board games and stuff. We had such a great time that it didn't really bother me when Dad had to leave to go back to work in Phoenix.

"I love you, Martin," he said, kissing me on the head. "I'll see you guys in a couple of weeks when you come out to Arizona."

"Yeah, Dad," I said, and bought a house for Park Place.

Chapter Twenty-Nine

I did stew quite a bit over Skunk being missing. He really was a great cat.

I decided you could do some things when you were angry that you could never undo. This, I felt, really was my fault.

That night, I had a little trouble going to sleep. I took out my book, and read about how the sons and daughters of the Australian convicts grew up honest and true. In the end, no one held them responsible for the crimes of their parents.

The next day, the day after Dad left, Farley and I were having waffles in the kitchen. Sunlight streamed through the windows. Mom was in a happy mood, smiling and laughing. The place smelled great. And I heard a meow at the door.

I jumped from my seat and opened the door.

In marched Skunk, carrying a tiny new kitten in his mouth. He went up the stairs to my room. I followed. He dropped the kitten in my closet, then turned around and marched back down the stairs and out the door.

He soon returned with another kitten, and another, and it started to dawn on me that maybe Skunk was not a he. *She* seemed to be the mother of seven kittens. And the whole family had taken up residence among my shoes.

Mom laughed until tears came to her eyes. Farley and I laughed, too. I felt happier than I ever remember feeling. I felt light and airy, as if a weight had been lifted off my chest and I could fly, or jump to the moon.

I decided that sometimes things just happened in this life that I didn't have anything to do with, that I wasn't responsible for. And Skunk's disappearance to have kittens was definitely one of those things.

When we had all calmed down and stopped laughing, Mom looked outside.

"I have an idea," she said. "It's bright, sunny and warm outside. Anybody want to go to the ocean?"

"Yeah!" said Farley. "Want to, Martin?"

"Let's go!" I said, charging up the stairs to get my stuff. "We'll dive through the waves like Dad showed us, swim out past where they're breaking, and ride them like a roller coaster! It'll be the best time we ever had!"

LET, LET, LET THE MAILMAN GIVE YOU COLD, CLAMMY

SHIVERS! SHIVERS! SHIVERS!!!

A Frightening Offer: Buy the first *Shivers* book at $3.99 and pick each additional book for only $1.99. Please include $2.00 for shipping and handling. Canadian orders: Please add $1.00 per book. (Allow 4-6 weeks for delivery.)

__ #1 The Enchanted Attic
__ #2 A Ghastly Shade of Green
__ #3 Ghost Writer
__ #4 The Animal Rebellion
__ #5 The Locked Room
__ #6 The Haunting House
__ #7 The Awful Apple Orchard
__ #8 Terror on Troll Mountain
__ #9 The Mystic's Spell
__ #10 The Curse of the New Kid
__ #11 Guess Who's Coming For Dinner?
__ #12 The Secret of Fern Island
__ #13 The Spider Kingdom
__ #14 The Curse in the Jungl
__ #15 Pool Ghoul
__ #16 The Beast Beneath the Boardwalk
__ #17 The Ghosts of Camp Massacre
__ #18 Your Momma's a Werewolf
__ #19 The Thing in Room 60
__ #20 Babyface and the Kille Mob
__ #21 A Waking Nightmare
__ #22 Lost in Dreamland
__ #23 Night of the Goat Boy
__ #24 Ghosts of Devil's Mars

I'm scared, but please send me the books checked above.

$__________ is enclosed.

Name____________________________________

Address__________________________________

City____________________ State________ Zip ________

Payment only in U.S. Funds. Please no cash or C.O.D.s
Send to: Paradise Press, 8551 Sunrise Blvd. #302, Plantation, FL 33322.